For grandma bears everywhere
~ A.R.

For Rosie, a most lovely grandma!
~ A.E.

tiger tales
5 River Road, Suite 128, Wilton, CT 06897
Published in the United States 2018
Originally published in Great Britain 2018
by Little Tiger Press
Text copyright © 2018 Alison Ritchie
Illustrations copyright © 2018 Alison Edgson
ISBN-13: 978-1-68010-079-2
ISBN-10: 1-68010-079-3
Printed in China
LTP/1400/1983/0817

For more insight and activities, visit us at www.tigertalesbooks.com

Me and My Grandma!

by Alison Ritchie • Illustrated by Alison Edgson

tiger tales

Me and my grandma
are ready to play.
We go on adventures
and stay out all day!

We race through the woods
to our favorite tree
And scramble up high—
there's a whole world to see!

We jump in the puddles
with splashes so high.
I hold my umbrella
and try to stay dry!

Grandma cartwheels downhill—
she's not scared at ALL.
I roll like a hedgehog
curled up in a ball.

We find special stones
to skip in the stream.
They bounce—plip, plip, plop.
We make such a good team!

If I tumble and fall,
Grandma squeezes me tight.
A bear hug from her
can make everything right.

We lie on the grass
and look up at the sky
To find funny shapes
in the clouds floating by.

If the weather is sunny,
we go for a swim.
Grandma dives like a pro
and I belly-flop in!

We love to go fishing,
just Grandma and me.
Side by side on the bridge
is right where we'll be.

As we head back toward home
in the soft evening light,
I count sleepy birds
tucked in safe for the night.

My grandma tells stories
(and I join in, too!)
About a small bear
and a grandma—guess who?

Me and my grandma
have the BEST time together.
I wish our adventures
could go on FOREVER!